KYLE'S LiTTLE SiSTER
KYLE'S LiTTLE SiSTER
KYLE'S LiTTLE SiSTER
KYLE'S LiTTLE SiSTER
KYLE'S LiTTLE SiSTER

KYLE'S LiTTLE SiSTER

Story & Art by

BonHyung Jeong

New York

KYLE'S LiTTLE SiSTER

BONHYUNG JEONG
LETTERING: JY EDITORIAL

This book is a work of fiction. Names, characters, places, and incidents are the product of the author's imagination or are used fictitiously. Any resemblance to actual events,locales, or persons, living or dead, is coincidental.

JY
150 West 30th Street, 19th Floor
New York, NY 10001

Visit us at jyforkids.com
facebook.com/jyforkids • twitter.com/jyforkids
jyforkids.tumblr.com • instagram.com/jyforkids

First JY Edition: June 2021

JY is an imprint of Yen Press, LLC.
The JY name and logo are trademarks of Yen Press, LLC.

Library of Congress Control Number: 2021934049

ISBNs: 978-1-9753-3589-2 (hardcover)
978-1-9753-1654-9 (paperback)
978-1-9753-3590-8 (ebook)

10 9 8 7 6 5 4 3 2 1

LSC-C

Printed in the United States of America

Table of Contents

CHAPTER 1

AT BIRTH
KYLE, LOOK WHO'S HERE!!
YOU'RE A BIG BROTHER NOW. CONGRATS!
I'M PRETTY SURE I KNEW THE MOMENT I WAS BORN THAT HE AND I WOULDN'T GET ALONG.
AGE 5
SO YOU'RE KYLE'S LITTLE SISTER! HOW CUTE!
AGE 7
That's Kyle's sister?!
She's nothing like him!
Shh!
AGE 9
I WAS HIS HOMEROOM TEACHER TOO!
I BET YOU'RE ALSO GOOD AT SPORTS!
HA-HA...
HE'S ALWAYS BEEN IN MY LIFE.
IN EVERY SINGLE MOMENT.
GRACE!
...CE!
NOT ONCE HAVE I BEEN FREE FROM BEING "KYLE'S LITTLE SISTER."

GRACE!
TIME TO GET UP!
WE'RE HERE!
I'M ALWAYS AMAZED AT HOW FAST YOU CAN FALL ASLEEP...
...HUH?
AWESOME! THANKS, MOM!
DON'T FORGET YOUR LUNCHES!
LCOME TO NGTON
DO I REALLY NEED TO TAKE THE BUS HOME?
CAN'T YOU PICK ME UP?
I TOLD YOU I'M BUSY TODAY. YOU HAVE TO GET USED TO THE BUS ANYWAY!
TODAY'S THE BIG DAY.
I'M GOING TO BE A SIXTH GRADER AT ELINGTON.

BYE, MOM!
SEE YOU LATER, SWEETIE.♥

VROOOM~...
ROOM 103...ROOM 103...
~~
~~
AMY: WE'RE AT THE FRONT ENTRANCE!

ON... M...Y... WA—
OW!

IT WAS NICE NOT HAVING YOU AROUND!
ARE WE IN THE SAME SCHOOL AGAIN?!
EXCEPT...I'LL BE WITH THIS "THING" AGAIN—MY BROTHER, KYLE BAILEY.

HA!
THAT'S MY LINE! I BET IT'S GONNA BE THE WORST YEAR EVER!
PFFT!

WHAT?!
YOU JUST JINXED YOURSELF, Y'KNOW.

IT'S ALL
HIS FAULT IF
SOMETHING DOES
GO WRONG!
THERE
SHE IS!
GRACE!
HE'S SUCH A...
OVER HERE!!!
AMY!!
JAY!!

YO-
WHAT'S UP?
GRACE! HOW ARE YOU? I MISSED YOU SO MUCH!!♥♥
Ouch..
AMY, WE HUNG OUT A WEEK AGO, REMEMBER...?
OW, OW...
OH...YEAH. I MEAN, WE COULD'VE HUNG OUT MORE, BUT YOU WERE TOO BUSY PLAYING THAT NEW GAME AND WOULDN'T COME OUT OF YOUR ROOM FOR THE NUMEROUS PLANS I MADE SPECIFICALLY FOR YOU.
S-SORRY...
I MEAN... I HEARD YOU GUYS HAD FUN!
H-HEY, JAY! HOW WAS YOUR WEEK?
HI, JAY.
HI...
HUH?

IT WAS FI—
WH-WHAT'S WITH THAT FACE?
AH! THE SWEET SCENT OF LOVE...
HOLD ON... I JUST THOUGHT OF THE PERFECT PLAN!
AMY ...!
HUH?
KYLE! THIS SATURDAY, LET'S CELEBRATE US GOING TO THE SAME SCHOOL AGAIN! PRETTY PLEASE?
STOP BOTHERING MY FRIEND!
NO! I HAVE PLANS WITH HIM THIS WEEKEND.
OW!
HA! I WASN'T ASKING YOU, MY STUPID BROTHER! I'M TRYING TO SET—
AMY!!

I TH-THINK I JUST SAW TERRY! DOESN'T HE STILL OWE YOU THAT BOOK?
OH YEAH!!
IT'S A SIGNED COPY! HE BETTER GIVE IT BACK!!
SORRY, MAN... WHY IS SHE SO ALL OVER THE PLACE...?
URRRGH...
DID YOU REALLY SEE TERRY?
I FEEL LIKE I'VE AGED FIFTY YEARS...
YOU KNOW HOW SHE IS, JAY—SHE'S BEEN LIKE THAT SINCE KINDERGARTEN!
PAT
PAT
SHE'S ALL ABOUT ROMANCE!
WELL, KINDA, I THINK... AHH, I REALLY SHOULDN'T HAVE MENTIONED ANYTHING TO HER...
LET'S GO!
COMING!
THEN YOU HAVE TO TALK TO HER ABOUT IT.
BUT SHE PROMISED ME SHE'D LAY OFF THIS TIME.
WHAT A WAY TO START THE MORNING...

WHAT'S YOUR FIRST CLASS?
HISTORY. YOU?
KYLE!
WOW!
HEY.
HOW WAS YOUR SUMMER?
EH, NOTHING SPECIAL.
HEY, HANNAH...
OH MY GOSH... IS THAT KYLE'S GIRLFRIEND?
NO, NO, HE DOESN'T HAVE ONE!
YO, KYLE! ANDREW!
KYLE~

WOW...
HA HA HA
YEAH... A CROWD IN NO TIME...
IT'S LIKE THEY'RE IN A WORLD OF THEIR OWN...
HEY, BY THE WAY, WHERE'S YOUR SISTER?
YEAH, DIDN'T YOU SAY SHE'S STARTING AT ELINGTON THIS YEAR?
RIGHT.
......
OH.
SHE'S OVER THERE.
H-HI...
HI!

BRIIINGN~
OH, THERE'S THE BELL.
GRACE, GET TO CLASS BEFORE THE SECOND BELL.
I KNOW ALREADY!
She doesn't really look like Kyle.
You think she'll do sports?
...
UGH. THEY'RE DEFINITELY KYLE'S FRIENDS.
KYLE'S REALLY POPULAR, HUH?
YEAH, AND IT SUCKS.
AWW...
LET'S GET TO CLASS. WONDER IF AMY GOT HER BOOK BACK.
HA-HA!
I DOUBT IT.
ALL RIGHT, CLASS!
WELCOME TO ELINGTON! I'M GOING TO BE YOUR HOMEROOM TEACHER.
EVEN IF IT'S THE SAME SCHOOL AS KYLE'S, STARTING A NEW SCHOOL IS EXCITING...

I'M SURE YOU'RE ALL EXCITED FOR YOUR FIRST DAY. PLEASE PASS THESE HANDOUTS BEHIND YOU...
I CAN'T BELIEVE I'M IN MIDDLE SCHOOL!
BLAH
BLAH
BLAH
BLAH

BRIIING~...

HEY, GUYS!
HEY, AMY!
LET'S HANG OUT AT MY PLACE! MY MOM'LL DROP YOU OFF LATER.
SOUNDS GOOD! LEMME JUST TELL MY MOM...

HA HA
HA
No way
HEE HEE
OMG!

HA
HA
HA
HA

HOW DO PEOPLE GET THAT OUTGOING?
I BET THEY'RE THE TYPE WHO GO TO PARTIES.
LET'S GO!

LIKES SPORTS
OUT-GOING
LIKES GAMES
QUIET
THEY SEEM MORE RELATED TO KYLE THAN I DO.

PFFT, WHATEVER.

GRACE, LET'S GET GOING! WE'RE GONNA MISS THE BUS!

MY DAD BAKED COOKIES LAST NIGHT!
SOOO...
ABOUT KYLE—
...
NUH-UH, AMY! I DON'T WANNA TALK ABOUT IT!
I TRY NOT TO GET INVOLVED WHEN IT COMES TO KYLE...
AWW, COME ON! DON'T BE SHY!
PING!
PING!
YOU ALMOST BLURTED IT OUT TO HIM THIS MORNING!
BUT IT GETS AWKWARD...
AMY...
...I...
HEAR ME OUT! ANDREW'S PLANNING A GAME NIGHT ON SATURDAY AND OF COURSE KYLE'S GONNA COME!
WE GIRLS WILL HAVE A SLEEPOVER ON THE SAME DAY! AND I'M SURE WE'LL ALL HANG OUT TOGETHER AT SOME POINT! THEN WHEN YOU HAVE A CHANCE, YOU CAN ASK KYLE FOR HIS PHONE NUMBER AND— BAM! YOU CAN START TEXTING HIM! AND ONCE YOU START TALKING, YOU CAN ASK HIM OUT, AND KYLE WILL NATURALLY START FALLING FOR YOU! I BET YOU GUYS'LL GET TOGETHER WITHIN THREE MONTHS!!! OH. MY. GODDD! I'M SO EXCITED!!
AMY...

I CAN'T BELIEVE JAY'S GONNA START DATING!!
KNOCK
KNOCK
I don't know what to say...
Ha-ha...
A GAME NIGHT WOULD BE FUN, THOUGH.

GIRLS, TIME TO GO HOME! I'LL DROP YOU OFF.
PERFECT TIMING!
THANK YOU!
THANK YOU!

HOW WAS SCHOOL, GUYS?
I'M GOING TO MAKE YOUR FAVORITE FOR DINNER, GRACE!

HI, MOM!
I'M HOME!
I HOPE AMY STOPS TRYING TO SET JAY UP...
HI, MOM.

REALLY? WHAT IS IT?
WANT TO GUESS?

STEAK?
BEEF STEW?
HOT DOGS?

IIIIIT'S CHICKEN PARMESAN WITH MAC AND CHEESE!
HUH?
I KNOW HOW MUCH YOU LIKE THEM!

DID I HEAR CHICKEN PARM?!
UH...
HA-HA. YES, YOU HEARD RIGHT!

CAN YOU MAKE ENOUGH FOR TOMORROW'S LUNCH?

WHY DON'T YOU HELP ME WITH THESE?
OKAY!
...
PRINCE CHARMING ALWAYS GETS THE ATTENTION...
BLAP-
HEYO, WAZZUP?
OH!
OHH!
I HEARD CHICKEN PARM, MOOOOM.

STUPID.

WHY DOES THE WORLD REVOLVE AROUND HIM?

KYLE'S LITTLE SISTER?
SHE DOESN'T REALLY LOOK LIKE KYLE.

I'LL MAKE CHICKEN PARMESAN WITH MAC AND CHEESE FOR YOU!
WHICH ARE KYLE'S FAVORITES!
MOM, YOU GAVE KYLE A RIDE FOR A WHOLE YEAR, BUT ALL I GET IS CHEESE THAT I DON'T EVEN LIKE?!

PFFT...
URGH.
BACK OFF.

GRACE!
DINNER'S
READY!
KNOCK
KNOCK!

GRACE?
*AHEM!
COMING!

GRACE!!
COMING!!

CHAPTER 2

BRIIING~...
~~
OKAY, CLASS, DON'T FORGET YOUR GROUP PROJECTS!
LET ME KNOW IF YOU HAVE ANY QUESTIONS.
BYE, MRS. CHUNG!

UM...
...MRS. CHUNG?
YES, AMY? HOW CAN I HELP YOU?

WELL...
I WAS HOPING I COULD SWITCH GROUPS...
PLEEEASE?

AWW...

SORRY, AMY, BUT...
...IF I LET YOU CHANGE YOUR GROUP, I'LL HAVE TO LET OTHERS DO IT TOO.
TSK!
WELL, AT LEAST YOU TRIED.
SOOO... NO.

CHATTER
CHATTER
WHO'S IN YOUR GROUP?
CHATTER
WENDY AND...
CHATTER

WA-
WA-
GRAAACE, LISTEN TO ME!

I'M LISTENING!
I MEAN, IT'S NOT FAIR!
WHY DO YOU TWO GET TO BE IN THE SAME GROUP?
BLAME MRS. CHUNG, NOT US!

OKAY, HOW ABOUT YOU CHOOSE WHICH BOARD GAME WE PLAY TODAY AT MY PLACE?
OH, HEY, YEAH!
HMM... WELL...

...AMY?
WELL, WHAT?
WELL, WHY DON'T WE GO TO MY PLACE **AND** I CHOOSE WHAT TO PLAY?

ANOTHER FAN CLUB?!

I MEAN, THEY JUST RELEASED THEIR SECOND ALBUM, SO I NEED MORE PEOPLE TO LISTEN TO THEIR SONGS!

WHAT HAPPENED TO THE DUDEZ?

I GUESS SHE SWITCHED...?

AND ALL THE MEMBERS ARE SUPER HANDSOME!

SO WHAT'S YOUR DECISION?

I WAS HOPING WE COULD PLAY THE NEW GAME I GOT...

YOUR PLACE...

MAYBE TOMORROW?

I WONDER IF THERE'S ANYONE WHO CAN WIN AGAINST AMY...
RUN INTO MY ARMS~♪
I NEED YOU~♬

YOU'RE SO COOL, JY!!
OH, AN UPDATE...

SO, JAY, WHAT KIND OF GAME DID YOU GET THIS TIME?

OH YEAH!
IT'S A STRATEGY CARD GAME THAT'S A TON OF FUN!

IT'S AN EXPANSION PACK OF THIS GAME...
OH, COOL!
...

GUYS, FOCUS! FOCUS AND APPRECIATE THEIR BEAUTY!

IF YOU'RE NOT GONNA PAY ATTENTION, WHAT'S THE POINT OF ME SHOWING IT TO YOU?!
OKAY, OKAY, WE'LL FOCUS!
BUT YOU'RE THE ONE WHO CHANGED THE PLAN...

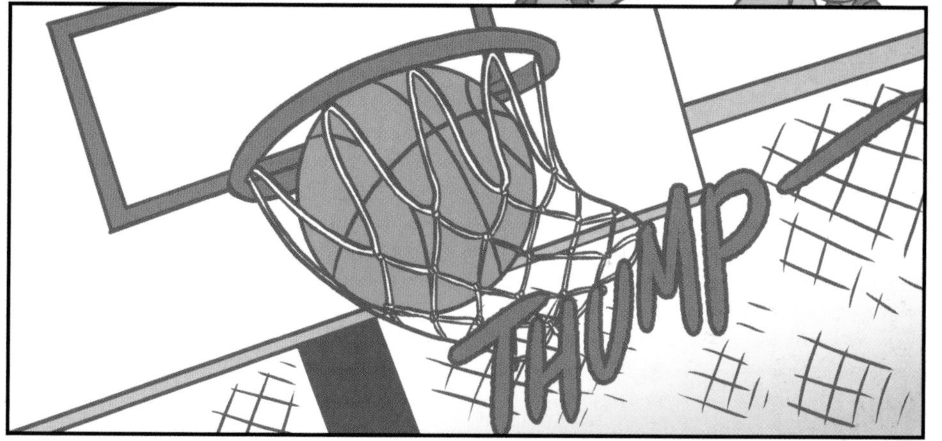
THUMP

YEAH!!
WOO-HOO-
GOOD JOB, GUYS

BYE!
BYE!
SEE YOU TOMORROW!

SO WHO'S COMING ON SATURDAY?
LET'S GET GOING.
IT'S GONNA BE YOU, ME, AND LIAM.
ACK, HEY!
WAIT, REALLY?
THAT'S IT?
YUP.
OR ALEX?
WHAT ABOUT JAKE?
THEY SAID THEY'RE BUSY...
OH, BUT YOUR SISTER'S COMING TOO!
LET GO, DUDE!
WHAT?!
Y-YOU INVITED GRACE...?
WHY WOULD YOU...?
OF COURSE NOT.

IT WASN'T ME...
LISTEN TO THIS...
IT WAS MY SISTER.
HEY, MOM?
YES, DEAR?
CAN MY FRIENDS SLEEP OVER ON SATURDAY TOO? PLEEEASE?
OF COURSE! IT'S GRACE AND JAY, RIGHT? IT'S BEEN A WHILE SINCE THEY'VE STAYED OVER.
DON'T I GET A SAY IN THIS...?
AND THAT'S WHAT HAPPENED.
YOU KNOW HOW IT GOES...
URGH...
GAAAH! WE'RE GONNA BE STUCK BABYSITTING FOR THE WHOLE NIGHT!
TELL ME ABOUT IT...

BUT I LIKE YOUR SISTERS! THEY'RE BOTH SO CUTE.
EWWW! WHY WOULD YOU EVER SAY THAT?
WHY NOT? I REALLY WISH I HAD A LITTLE SIBLING...
DUDE, YOU REALLY DON'T...
YEAH, BE GRATEFUL YOU DON'T.
IT'S SO ANNOYING BEING THE BIG BROTHER!
THEY DON'T LISTEN...
I'M ALWAYS RESPONSIBLE IF SOMETHING HAPPENS...
IT'S LIKE SHE WAS BORN TO CAUSE TROUBLE FOR ME!
HE CAN'T UNDERSTAND OUR PAIN...
OLDER BROTHER CLUB
BUT I KNOW THAT, DEEP DOWN, YOU STILL REALLY CARE FOR THEM.
HOW SWEET!
UGH!
NO WAY!
I CAN'T WAIT FOR SATURDAY!
HNNNNGH...

GAME NIGHT
AMY: I'M SO EXCITED!!! YOU READY, JAY? EVERYTHING WILL WORK OUT IF WE JUST STICK TO THE PLAN!!!
JAY: ...
GEEZ...IS AMY REALLY GONNA TRY SOMETHING TONIGHT...?
NOT SURE IF I SHOULD STOP HER OR NOT...
JAY IS TYPING...
WE STILL GOTTA FINISH THE BOSS FIGHT, RIGHT?
ANDREW: YUP! BTW, YOU GUYS GOOD WITH PINEAPPLE PIZZA? :D
LIAM: YEAAAAH!
GROOOOOSS!!
LIAM: LOOOL
ANDREW: TOO LATE!
OKAY, GUYS, HAVE FUN!
CALL ME IF YOU NEED ME TO PICK YOU UP, OKAY?
'KAAAY!!

GAME NIGHT
WHY DON'T YOU JUST RIDE BACK WITH MOM AND SAVE HER A TRIP?
HA! IF I GO HOME, I'M TAKING YOU WITH ME!
PSST!
Jay! Go sit next to him!
WHOA, GRACE IS SO GOOD!
HA! I GUESS...

I'm fine over here...
Tsk. okay...

OMG! GRACE, YOU'RE AMAZING!
WHY DOES IT FEEL LIKE SOMEONE'S WATCHING ME...?

AMY! STOP PUSHING ME...!
SORRYYY! JUST TRYING TO SEE...
ACK! DARN YOU, LIAM!
HEH!
CHIPS

KIDS, THE FOOD'S HERE!
THANKS, DAD!

PIZZA!
YEE-HA!
PIZZAS
PIZZAS
CHIPS

COKE!
EXCUSE ME—!!
THONK
!!
SPLASH
WHOA!
UH.....

I'M S-SO SORRY, KYLE!
IT'S FINE. IT'S JUST COKE.
YES!
DID YOU GET ANY ON YOU?
WANNA BORROW A SHIRT?
YES PLEASE.

CAN I USE YOUR WASHER?
SURE.
SEE? HE SAID IT'S OKAY!

...
HEE-HEE! NOW YOU HAVE SOMETHING TO TALK TO HIM ABOUT!

HMM... IT...
IT SORT OF FEELS LIKE AMY CROSSED THE LINE THIS TIME...

OKAY, OKAY, I'LL GO TALK TO HIM.
PROMISE ME YOU WILL!
I HOPE SHE DOESN'T GO ANY FURTHER.

HA-HA-HA!

WHAT'S SO FUNNY, GUYS?
LET ME SEE!

!

HA HA HA HA

HA HA HA HA
...
BEST GAME NIGHT EVER!
I'M SO GLAD I REMEMBERED I HAD IT!
HA HA HA
OMG, ANDREW, YOU'RE BRILLIANT!

AH...?

OH HEY...
Jay, tell him he's cute!

I don't know... I really don't think that's a good idea...

Huh?! C'mon, this is your chance!

HA
HA
HA
HA
B-but...
...I...
Hurry!

BA-DUMP
BA-DUMP
BA-DUMP

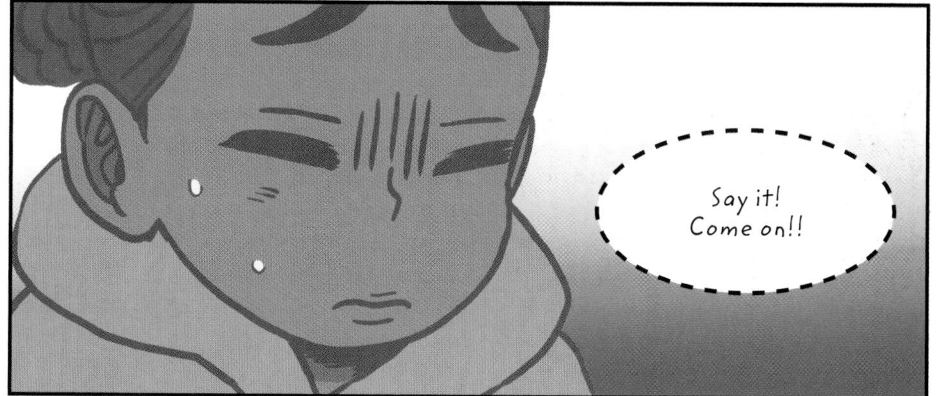
Say it! Come on!!

STOP IT!!

H-HUH?

S-SORRY...
UM... JAY?
I'M...
...JUST GONNA GO TO BED.
YOU GUYS HAVE FUN.
S-SO...
WANT A TURN, LIAM?
W-WAIT, JAY...!

CHAPTER 3

KNOCK!
KNOCK!
SWEETIE?
I BROUGHT YOU SOME BREAKFAST...
LET ME TURN THE LIGHTS ON.
ARE YOU FEELING ANY BETTER?
...I GUESS...

SO...
...DO YOU WANT TO TELL ME WHAT HAPPENED?

'KAY...

LAST NIGHT
JAY!

JAY...
...ARE YOU OKAY?

S-SORRY...
...BUT I THINK...
I THINK I JUST WANT TO GO HOME...

JAY, WHAT WAS THAT ABOUT?!
AMY...

I...I REALLY DON'T WANT TO TALK ABOUT IT RIGHT NOW...
NO! WE ARE GONNA TALK ABOUT THIS NOW! WHAT EXACTLY IS YOUR PROBLEM?!
G-GUYS...
C'MON, TELL ME!
Y-YOU...YOU'RE SO DRAMATIC ABOUT EVERYTHING!
I KNOW YOU'RE TRYING TO HELP, BUT...
...THEY'RE MY FEELINGS! IT'S SERIOUS TO ME!
S-SO PLEASE STOP TAKING IT SO LIGHTLY AND PUSHING ME AROUND!

...ARE YOU SAYING
I'M JUST DOING THIS
FOR FUN?
WHAT...?
N-NO! THAT'S NOT—!
I'M JUST ASKING YOU TO GIVE ME SOME SPACE!
HA! YOU NEVER DO ANYTHING ON YOUR OWN!
AND YOU KNOW WHAT?
IF YOU WEREN'T GRACE'S FRIEND...
KYLE WOULDN'T HAVE NOTICED SOMEONE SO TIMID LIKE YOU!
...HE WOULDN'T EVEN KNOW YOU EXIST!
AMY! YOU'RE GOING TOO FAR!
WHAT? I'M JUST TELLING THE TRUTH!
LET'S GO, JAY. I'LL WALK YOU HOME.

HMPH. SINCE WHEN DID YOU CARE ABOUT JAY, GRACE?
HUH?!
AT LEAST I TRIED TO HELP. WHAT DID YOU DO?
YOU THINK JAY'S NOT GOOD ENOUGH FOR YOUR PRECIOUS BROTHER.
WH- WHAT?!
WHY WOULD SHE SAY SUCH A...?!
THAT'S CRAZY!
YOU KNOW WHAT? COOL YOUR HEAD UNTIL I GET BACK, AND THEN WE CAN—
GRACE...
IT'S FINE...
I THINK I'LL JUST GO HOME BY MYSELF.
B-BUT... JAY!

. . .
WELL, ARE YOU HAPPY NOW?
YOU GOT HER MAD AT ME TOO!

WHY WOULD YOU SAY SOMETHING LIKE THAT?!
YOU BETTER FIGURE OUT WHAT TO DO, 'COS I'M NOT CLEANING UP YOUR MESS THIS TIME!
...WHATEVER. I DON'T WANT YOUR HELP ANYWAY.

UGH. SO THAT'S HOW SHE'S GONNA BE?
HMPH!

YOU KNOW...
...I'M ONLY FRIENDS WITH YOU 'COS OF OUR BROTHERS ANYWAY.

...GRACE!
WHAT ARE YOU DOING HERE ALONE?
WHERE'S JAY? DID SHE GO HOME?
AND WHERE'S AMY?
GRACE? YOU OKAY...?
wann' g'hm...
WHAT?
I SAID I WANNA GO HOME, STUPID!
WAAAHHHHHHH
GEEZ, OKAY. I'LL CALL MOM...
WAHHHH
AWW, HONEY, I'M SORRY...
YEAH...

PEK
WELL, IF YOU'RE DONE WITH HOMEWORK, YOU CAN STAY IN BED A BIT LONGER.
HAVE SOME BREAKFAST, AND—
OH! IT'S YOUR DAD.
RING
GET SOME REST, OKAY, GRACE?
TELL ME IF YOU NEED ANYTHING.
THANKS, MOM...
HI, HONEY! HOW'S THE WEATHER OVER THERE?
GOOD TO HEAR!
THE KIDS? THEY'RE DOING WELL...
NO, DAD. I HAD THE WORST NIGHT EVER.
THUMP
BLAAARGH...
RUSTLE
RUSTLE

FOUND IT!

NO TEXTS...

SHOULD I MESSAGE JAY...?

TAP
HOW...
...ARE YOU DOING...?
TAP
TAP
HMM... NO, NO.
TAP

HEY, JAY!
WAIT, NO EXCLAMATION MARK.
I'M SO SORRY.
I SWEAR I NEVER SAID ANYTHING...
...LIKE THAT.
AAAGH!

...

HERE... SORRY, MOM.
NO PROBLEM, HONEY. I WAS JUST ABOUT TO DO LAUNDRY ANYWAY.
THANKS...
YO, GRACE!

CATCH!
FWIP
OH!

DON'T START, YOU TWO.
OOPS...
TOO FAST FOR YOU?

WHACK
WHACK
SWING—
. . .
THAT'S ENOUGH, BOTH OF YOU!
PUNCH!
WHOSE FAULT DOES HE THINK IT IS THAT I'M IN THIS SITUATION?
KYLE IS THE SOURCE OF ALL MY PROBLEMS IN LIFE.
I'M ONLY FRIENDS WITH YOU 'COS OF OUR BROTHERS ANYWAY.
REALLY? YOU COULDN'T HAVE SAID ANYTHING ELSE?!
BLEEEEH!
GRACE, I KNOW YOU'RE UPSET RIGHT NOW, BUT YOU CAN'T TAKE IT OUT ON YOUR BROTHER!
HAS TONS TO SAY BUT SWALLOWS THE WORDS

UGH...I'M EXHAUSTED...

NO NEW MESSAGES

GUESS I'LL JUST PLAY SOME GAMES...

MONDAY
BRIIING~

SNEAK~..

PHEW...

I DON'T WANT TO LET ANYONE SEE ME EAT ALONE...
I WONDER WHERE AMY AND JAY ARE EATING LUNCH...
ESPECIALLY NOT KYLE AND HIS GROUP...

JAY WOULDN'T EVEN LOOK IN MY DIRECTION...

...AMY KEPT TO HERSELF...

...AND I'M EATING LUNCH ALONE.
MUNCH...
MONCH

IS THIS HOW MIDDLE SCHOOL IS GONNA BE?
HMM... I'LL FINISH MY SANDWICH LATER.
AH...THIS PLACE IS NICE AND QUIET...

IS OUR FRIENDSHIP REALLY OVER?
CRACK~

HOW AM I GOING TO DO THE SCIENCE PROJECT WITH JAY LIKE THIS?
THIS REALLY SUCKS...

HA
HA
HA
HA
OH SHOOT, IT'S KYLE!

SO, SO, SO ANNOYING...
WHY DO THEY ALWAYS HAVE TO BE IN SUCH A BIG CROWD? IT'S LIKE THEY'RE A SCHOOL OF FISH...

HMPH. WHATEVER.

HE'S PROBABLY NEVER HAD TO EAT LUNCH ALONE IN HIS LIFE...

OH!

HOPE I DON'T SOUND AWKWARD.

H-HI, JAY!

UH...

...H-HI...

?!

UNBELIEVABLE.

WHAT DID I EVER DO TO DESERVE THAT?
NOTHING!

IT'S NOT LIKE I WAS THE ONE WHO SAID ALL THOSE THINGS.

FINE, IF THAT'S HOW THEY'RE GONNA BE...

...I'M DONE THINKING ABOUT EITHER OF THEM.

I'M BETTER OFF BEING ALONE.

MUNCH...
MONCH

CHAPTER 4

HIT 4500!
ARGH
HHHHH
HIT 3500!
HIT 2500!

...

HEY, UH... DON'T YOU HAVE ANY PLANS FOR TODAY?
PLANS? WHAT PLANS?

Y'KNOW, PLANS TO HANG OUT WITH JAY AND AMY?

IT'S BEEN A WEEK.
OH... UM...
WE DON'T TALK ANYMORE.

IT'S BEEN A WEEK SINCE I'VE STARTED GOING TO CLASS ALONE...

...EATING LUNCH ALONE...
MUNCH
MUNCH

...AND DOING HOMEWORK ALONE.

AND I'M TOTALLY FINE WITH THAT.
WHY DO YOU WANNA KNOW?
I MEAN...I WAS THERE THAT NIGHT, SO I WAS JUST WONDERING IF YOU GUYS WERE OKAY.
WE'RE OKAY. THERE, HAPPY?

WELL THEN, GUESS YOU'RE ALL ALONE ON A SUNDAY 'COS YOU'RE SUCH A LOSER.

TYPICAL GRACE—NO WONDER PEOPLE DON'T WANT TO HANG OUT WITH...

Bonk!
...YOU—

HEY! WHAT WAS THAT FOR...?!

WHAM!
...!

WHAT'D YOU CALL ME? A LOSER? "TYPICAL GRACE"?!
I SAID I WAS SORRY!
OW!
OW, HEY! QUIT IT!
GRACE! YOUNG LADY, STOP IT RIGHT NOW!
OW!
KICK
KICK
KICK

YOU CAN'T HIT YOUR BRO—
BUT HE STARTED IT!

OKAY, THAT'S IT. YOU'RE GROUNDED FOR THE DAY!
FINE!

DON'T YOU TAKE THAT TONE WITH ME, GRACE BAILEY!

I SAID, "FINE"!

I'M...GONNA GO TO ANDREW'S...

LET ME GET OUT OF HERE.

BAM

SIGH--

STUPID KYLE!

MY MOM ALWAYS...

TAP

TAP

...TAKES HIS SIDE.

TAP

TAP

OH.

GUUUUUH...
CHIN UP, GRACE! DON'T WASTE TIME SULKING!
I WAS DOING FINE ALL WEEK BY MYSELF. I'M FINE!
SLAP!
SLAP!!
HAAAH...
NEW_KID123 AND OTHERS
SELFIE WITH FRIENDS.
#SCHOOL #NEWSCHOOL #BFF
#BEST FRIENDS FOREVER
I WISH I DIDN'T GO TO THE SAME SCHOOL AS KYLE...
MAYBE THEN WE WOULDN'T HAVE HAD A FIGHT IN THE FIRST PLACE.

IT'S WEIRD NOT BEING WITH THEM... I USUALLY SPEND THE WEEKEND AT ONE OF THEIR HOUSES...
SEVENTY DROPPED A NEW SINGLE?
NEVER THOUGHT I'D MISS AMY'S FANGIRLING...
?
HM? TODAY'S MEMORY PHOTO?
OH...
CLASS OF
GRADUATION
I REALLY DO HAVE A LOT OF MEMORIES WITH THEM.
HUH...I DON'T REMEMBER TAKING THIS...
I BET AMY TOOK IT.
56

56
...BUT I GUESS WE WON'T BE MAKING NEW ONES.

CLASS O
DELETE THIS POST?
CANCEL

HAAAAH...

I'M ACTUALLY NOT FINE AT ALL.

GRRRRR
RRRR
1SHOT
2SHOT
3SHOT

SHOOT 'EM!
PING—!
SHOOM—
LEFT! ON YOUR LEFT!
HAH! GOTCHA!

TA-LA-
LA-
LA-
MISSION COMPLETE
YEAAAH!
WE DID IT!

HEY, HEY! I WANNA PLAY TOO!

AMY...
DON'T YOU HAVE ANY PLANS TODAY?
NOPE! SO IS IT MY TURN?
WAAAAAAA~
DAD! ANDREW HIT ME!!
YOU SURE IT'S OKAY? SHE'S CRYING PRETTY HARD...
SHE'S JUST BEING DRAMATIC. BESIDES, SHE WON'T LEAVE US ALONE OTHERWISE.
WAAAA
SHE'S BEING SO CLINGY AGAIN. SHE'S BEEN EATING LUNCH WITH US TOO!
SPEAKING OF...
HMM?
WHAT'S GRACE DOING?
SHE'S AT HOME.

DANG...YOU THINK THEY'RE STILL FIGHTING?
YEAH, PROBABLY...

YOU THINK WE SHOULD DO ANYTHING ABOUT IT?

HUH? US? WHY SHOULD WE?
THIS IS THEIR PROBLEM, NOT OURS.
URGH... I STILL FEEL LIKE WE SHOULD DO SOMETHING...
AW, YOU WORRIED ABOUT AMY?

NO! IT'S JUST THAT'S THE ONLY WAY TO STOP HER FROM FOLLOWING ME AROUND.
HAH! SUCKS TO BE YOU.
READY FOR THE NEXT STAGE?

OH, AMY!
IS ANDREW
BEING MEAN
AGAIN?
GAH!
GET
'EM!

DO YOU
WANT TO HELP
DAD MAKE
SANDWICHES?

NO...
I'LL JUST
BE IN MY
ROOM.

CLASS OF 2

CLASS OF
GRADUATION

DRIP...

...I'M SO, SO SORRY...

GRACE! DINNERTIME!
KYLE SAID HE'S GOING TO EAT AT ANDREW'S.
HMM...? SHE REALLY WENT ALL OUT...
SO IT'S JUST THE TWO OF US FOR TONIGHT.
THANKS FOR THE FOOD.
LOOK AT THAT BEDHEAD...DID YOU HAVE A NICE NAP?

...THE STEAK TASTES BETTER THAN USUAL...

THERE'S SECONDS IF YOU WANT.
I'M GOOD.

BRUSH YOUR TEETH... AND DON'T STAY UP TOO LATE!
YES, MOM.

I FEEL A LOT BETTER AFTER DINNER AND A NAP.
I SHOULD CHECK MY HOMEWORK.

SPROING!!
IMPORTA
• RESEARCH CH. I SCIENCE CLASS G DUE MONDAY.
*IT'S CURRENTLY SUNDAY.

OH NOOOOOO!
GRACE, BE QUIET!

CHAPTER 5

ALL RIGHT, CLASS! PLEASE GET TOGETHER WITH YOUR GROUPS.
REMEMBER, YOUR PROJECT PROPOSALS ARE DUE NEXT WEEK.
COME UP AND TALK TO ME IF YOU HAVE ANY PROBLEMS.
HEY—..
OH, EXCUSE...
...ME...

SHOOT...

RIGHT... WE'RE IN THE SAME GROUP.

HOPE IT'LL BE OKAY.
HEY!

SO DID YOU GUYS FINISH YOUR PARTS?
YUP!

I WENT AHEAD AND LOOKED UP THE PEOPLE—
WAIT, WHAT?

?
YOU WERE SUPPOSED TO SUMMARIZE WHAT'S IN THE TEXTBOOK.
HUH?

I DON'T REMEMBER THAT AT ALL...

B-BUT...

...I...

"I..." WHAT?

WHOA THERE, TOM.

IT'S FINE. WE'VE STILL GOT A WEEK TO GET IT DONE.

IF GRACE CAN FINISH THE SUMMARY BY FRIDAY, WE CAN MEET UP DURING THE WEEKEND TO DO THE PROPOSAL...
...AND THEN FIGURE OUT THE PRESENTATION DURING CLASS NEXT WEEK.
HMM...
...GUESS THAT WORKS.
THEN IT'S SETTLED! CAN YOU GIVE ME YOUR NUMBER, GRACE? YOU CAN TEXT ME WHEN YOU'RE DONE WITH YOUR SECTION.
O-OKAY!

HERE YOU GO.
...
......
HANG ON, YOUR LAST NAME IS BAILEY?
YUP, THAT'S ME.
DO YOU WANNA GRAB LUNCH TOGETHER?
UM...
YEAH, SURE!
OH, AND I PROMISE, I'LL GET IT DONE ON TIME.
BRIIING~..

SO WHAT DO YOU DO IN YOUR FREE TIME?
THERE'S THIS POPULAR NEW GAME...
OH, THE OPEN-WORLD ONE?
DO YOU PLAY TOO? THAT'S SO COOL! I JUST UNLOCKED CO-OP MODE, SO DO YOU WANNA GAME AFTER WE FINISH THE PROJECT THIS WEEKEND?
REALLY? YES! I'M TOTALLY DOWN!
WHO'S YOUR FAVORITE CHARACTER?
OOH, GOOD QUESTION. I JUST MET...
OH WAIT! LUNCH IS ALMOST OVER!
WOW, SHE'S REALLY ENERGETIC...
COME WITH ME. I KNOW THE BEST SPOT.
O-OKAY.

I NEVER THOUGHT OF HAVING LUNCH HERE.
LET'S SIT HERE!
I'M SURE THIS IS WHERE KYLE HANGS OUT...

BUT I THINK I'VE MADE A NEW FRIEND!
SO WHICH ELEMENTARY SCHOOL DID YOU GO TO?
ME? I—

I'M GETTING SOME STRONG AMY VIBES...
WE DEFINITELY DIDN'T GO TO THE SAME SCHOOL, RIGHT? IT'S SO AWESOME THAT WE GET TO MAKE NEW FRIENDS NOW. THERE ARE A FEW PEOPLE FROM MY ELEMENTARY SCHOOL HERE TOO! LIKE SASHA, SHE'S ALSO IN OUR SCIENCE CLASS...
AH...THAT'S COOL...

BY THE WAY, DO YOU HAVE ANY SIBLINGS?
YEAH... THAT'S MY OLDER BROTHER OVER THERE.
OMIGOSH, KYLE BAILEY IS YOUR BROTHER?
EVERYONE IN SCHOOL KNOWS WHO HE IS!
HE'S SO HANDSOME. I'M SO JEALOUS YOU HAVE SUCH A COOL BROTHER!

I-I DON'T THINK HE'S THAT GREAT...
WHO'S SHE? WHY'S SHE STICKING SO CLOSE TO HIM?
WAIT... HUH?
...
I'M ONLY FRIENDS WITH YOU 'COS OF OUR BROTHERS.
DUNNO. SHE SUCKS.
DON'T KNOW, HUH?
CAN I ASK WHAT HAPPENED?
WH- WHAT?

NO...I-IT'S SORT OF PERSONAL...

...

OKAY, FINE. BUT YOU CAN'T TELL ANYBODY.
I SWEAR!

WE USED TO BE FRIENDS, BUT...
BUT?
BASICALLY, SHE TOLD ME THAT SHE'S ONLY FRIENDS WITH ME 'COS OUR BROTHERS ARE FRIENDS.

OMIGOSH... THAT'S AWFUL!

THAT'S WAY OVER THE LINE!
I BET SHE NEVER THOUGHT OF YOU AS A FRIEND IF SHE COULD SAY SOMETHING LIKE THAT.
Y-YOU THINK SO?

BRIIIING~...
YEAH!
AH, THERE'S THE BELL.
OH.
HI, CAM!
HEY, HOW'S IT GOING?
WHAT'S UP, CAM?
HERE, GRACE, WATCH THIS.
OUCH!
BUMP!

SCATTER—

...
WHOOPS. SORRY!

HA
HA
HA
HA
HA
HA

BRRIIIING...

I KNOW WHAT CAM DID WAS MEAN, BUT...
THAT'S WHAT YOU GET...
...I THINK AMY DESERVED IT.

IT'S HER FAULT WE'RE NOT TOGETHER ANYMORE.

CAM PROBABLY DID IT FOR ME...

LIKE CAM SAID, IF AMY REALLY THOUGHT OF ME AS A FRIEND...

...SHE WOULDN'T HAVE SAID SUCH A THING.
HEY, GRACE!

HEY.
I'LL TEXT YOU LATER, OKAY?
BYE, GRACE!

MOM! I'M HOME!
HEY, SWEETIE! GRACE, TURN OFF YOUR GAME, IT'S DINNERTIME!
DING!
NEW FRIEND REQUEST

DING!

BT&B
10:45 PM
NEW FOLLOWING
CAMTHEFRECKLE
STARTED FOLLOWING YOU.
+ JIMMY.K, ASHELY SUGAR AND 3 OTHERS ARE FOLLOWING THIS...

ONE NEW MESSAGE FROM CAM

HEY, LET'S EAT LUNCH TOMORROW!
I'LL BRING A FRIEND!
SURE, SOUNDS GOOD!

GUESS I WON'T HAVE TO EAT ALONE ANYMORE...

CHAPTER 6

GRACE!

OVER HERE!

WHAT'S UP?
HEY, GRACE!
THANKS FOR SAVING ME A SEAT.

I HAVE A NEW GROUP OF FRIENDS.

CAM'S POPULAR...

...AND LIKES THE SAME GAMES I DO.

BUT...

LOOK WHO IT IS.

EW, DO YOU SMELL SOMETHING FUNKY?

OMIGOSH, YEAH! I BET IT'S COMING FROM HER.

AH-HA-HA! GROSS!

DURING CLASS

AMY STEWART, EYES ON YOUR OWN TEST!

LUNCHTIME
CHICKEN NUGGETS FOR ME, PLEASE!
OOOH! THEY'VE GOT PIZZA!
ARE YOU SERIOUS...?

DID YOU SEE THE NEW TRAILER?

THERE'S THAT NEW DONUT SHOP...
BUMP!

HEY, WATCH WHERE YOU'RE GOING!
HERE, AMY.

HEY!!!
OOH, HOW SCARY.
HA-HA!

THE HECK? AMY, DO YOU KNOW THEM?
UM...
N-NO...

HAH! DID YOU SEE THE LOOK ON HER FACE?

OW!

HEY, WATCH...
...IT...
BLUSH—...
OH...
SORRY ABOUT THAT...
N-NO, IT'S TOTALLY FINE, KYLE! NO WORRIES!
UM...
HAVE WE MET BEFORE...?
OH! WELL, NOT YET...
FIDGET
FIDGET
HUH...UM, OKAY...?
THEN WHY DO YOU KNOW MY NAME...?
KYLE, HOLD THEM!
ACK!
ANDREW?
DUDE, YOU JUST LET THEM GET AWAY!
RUN, RUN!

THEY BUMPED INTO AMY AND GOT MILK ALL OVER HER, BUT THEY RAN OFF WITHOUT APOLOGIZING!
WHAT?! IS AMY OKAY?
LOOKS LIKE THE COAST IS CLEAR.
HUFF
HUFF
ARGH, THAT GUY RUINED MY CHANCE TO TALK TO KYLE!
UGH, I KNOW...
I MISSED MY MOMENT TO PASS BY.
BUT THAT AMY GIRL IS ALWAYS EATING WITH THE EIGHTH GRADERS. THINK SHE'S DATING ONE OF THEM?
YEAH, I BET THAT WAS HER BOYFRIEND.
...

HE PISSES ME OFF! I'M GONNA REPORT HIM TO A TEACHER IF HE CHASES AFTER US AGAIN.
THAT'S PROBABLY ANDREW...
BY THE WAY, HOW LONG ARE YOU GONNA HANG OUT WITH GRACE?
HM? OH.
I MEAN...
SHE'S KYLE'S SISTER, SO I'VE GOTTA BE NICE TO HER, RIGHT?
PFF—
WHY ELSE WOULD I HANG OUT WITH HER.
PFFT...I FEEL SORRY FOR HER NOW.
HA-HA! SERIOUSLY, SHE'S SUCH A NERD.
BRIIING~
...
OH, LET'S GET GOING. WE HAVE MATH NEXT, RIGHT?

BRIIING~...
SURE, I'M IN!
WANNA GO GET FROYO WITH US?
GRACE?
YES? OH...
UM... H-HEY.
S-SO...
...CAN WE TALK?
AHEM!
I DON'T THINK THIS IS ABOUT THE PROJECT...
UH...YEAH, SURE. JUST A SEC.
...AND I HOPE IT'S NOT ABOUT KYLE.

WHAT COULD IT BE ABOUT...?
HEY.

DO YOU WANNA...
I HAVE PLANS, SO...

OH...

UM...WELL, IT'S ABOUT AMY...
NO, STOP. I DON'T WANT TO TALK ABOUT HER.

...
OKAY, FINE. THAT'S FAIR. JUST...
...COULD YOU TELL CAM TO STOP BEING MEAN TO HER?

I DON'T KNOW WHAT YOU'RE TALKING ABOUT.
AND IF YOU WANT TO TALK ABOUT PEOPLE BEING MEAN—

GRACE.

I KNOW AMY SAID SOME AWFUL THINGS, BUT...

...AREN'T WE ALL FRIENDS?
YOU KNOW THIS ISN'T RIGHT.

CAN'T WE... CAN'T WE GO BACK TO HOW WE USED TO BE?

...I...
GRACE!

SORRY TO INTERRUPT, BUT WE'VE GOT PLANS.

IS IT EVEN POSSIBLE FOR US GO BACK TO HOW WE WERE BEFORE?

I'VE GOT GRACE! LET'S GO, GUYS!

IT FEELS LIKE IT'S TOO LATE FOR THAT.

SWEETHEART, JAY'S HERE!
H-HI.

GOOD MORNING!
CHATTER
CHATTER
HA HA
CHATTER

CHATTER
CHATTER
HA
HA
HA
HA

TAP!

GOOD MORNING.

M-MORNING, JAY!
DID YOU FINISH THE HISTORY REPORT YET?
YUP! I HAVE TO PRINT IT OUT AT THE LIBRARY.

CHAPTER 7

LED BY CAM, THE PRESENTATION WENT WELL.
~~
~~

JAY AND I HAVEN'T TALKED TO EACH OTHER ABOUT ANYTHING OTHER THAN THE PRESENTATION.

ANY QUESTIONS?

GOOD JOB, GUYS. OKAY, WHO'S NEXT?
WANNA HANG AFTER SCHOOL?
YEAH!

HA HA HA
HA

I'M STILL EATING LUNCH WITH CAM'S GROUP, BUT...
...NOT SURE WHAT THEY'RE TALKING ABOUT...

HI! MIND IF I SIT HERE?
OH, NOT AT ALL.
SHE'S NEW...

I'M AUDREY! IT'S NICE TO MEET YOU.
...
??
NICE TO MEET YOU TOO!

HEY, AUDREY. BEAT IT.
CAN'T YOU SEE WE'RE IN THE MIDDLE OF A CONVERSATION?

!
O-OH, SORRY...
UM...

PFFT.
WHO INVITED THAT LOSER?

WHAT WAS THAT ALL ABOUT?

I THOUGHT SHE SEEMED NICE...

I'M SURE CAM HAD A REASON FOR SAYING THAT.

HEY! STEWART!

...WHAT?

...
OH. HI, JAY. CAN I TALK TO AMY FOR A SEC?

...

SORRY. WE HAVE TO GO GET SOMETHING FROM OUR LOCKERS.
LET'S GO. YOUR LOCKER'S KIND OF FAR, RIGHT?
Y-YEAH.
SEE YOU IN CLASS.
WH-WHEN DID THOSE TWO GET CLOSE AGAIN...?
WHAT'S HER PROBLEM?

THAT'S ANNOYING.
WHATEVER.
I DON'T HANG OUT WITH THEM ANYMORE ANYWAY.
STILL, HOW CAN JAY FORGIVE HER FOR WHAT SHE SAID?
LET'S GO, GRACE.
DURING SCHOOL.
AFTER SCHOOL.

THEY'RE...

...ALWAYS...

...TOGETHER.
JUST IGNORE THEM...

GRACE?

OH, WHOOPS.

NOTHING.

?

S...

SORRY, WHAT WERE YOU SAYING?

HAAH... HOME SWEET HOME...
FWUMP...
MY HEAD FEELS LIKE IT'S GONNA EXPLODE...
STOP THINKING ABOUT IT, GRACE! STOP THINKING!
AGH, WHY ARE THINGS SO COMPLICATED?
BUT I CAN'T GET IT OUT OF MY MIND...
Hmm-...
HEY, GRACE!
COME ON IN, GUYS!

POP!

I BROUGHT THE GAME!

LOOK! THERE'S SODA! CAN WE DRINK IT?
HELP YOURSELVES!

MOM'S GONNA BE LATE TODAY, SO WE CAN TAKE OVER THE LIVING ROOM.
!
BUT I WAS HERE FIRST...

PUSH!
GO TO YOUR ROOM, WHY DON'T YOU? SCRAM.

ALL RIGHT, ALL RIGHT, FINE!
GREAT, BYE!

AREN'T YOU GOING OVER TO MY HOUSE WITH JAY AND AMY?

OH YEAH, YOU CAN GO THERE.
THEY SAID THEY'LL BE THERE FOR A WHILE.
...
UM...

...WE'RE STILL NOT TALKING...
...OH.
SILENCE

DO...
DO YOU WANNA HANG WITH US, THEN?
WHAT?! NO!
UGH, THOSE TWO!

THANKS, LIAM, BUT I THINK I'LL PASS SO SOMEONE ELSE HAS A CHANCE TO WIN.
HAH! SAYS THE LOSER.

WHAT THE HECK IS HIS PROBLEM?!
LET ME TELL YOU SOMETHING.
WHAT?

JUST SUCK IT UP AND DEAL WITH IT.
I BET YOU GOT MAD OVER SOMETHING STUPID, SO GET OVER IT.

YOU DON'T KNOW ANY—
"YOU DON'T KNOW ANYTHING"? PLEASE, I'VE KNOWN YOU YOUR WHOLE LIFE.
HA-HA!
MAYBE YOU SHOULD LAY OFF...

IF AMY AND JAY ARE FINE NOW, THAT MEANS...
...YOU'RE THE PROBLEM.
ANGER GAGE

YOU KNOW, IF YOU KEEP BEING STUBBORN...
GRAB—...
...YOU'LL END UP ALONE WITHOUT ANY FRIENDS—

WHACK!!!
THUD
OW!
POW
POW
WHAM
STOP!
THUD
POW
WHAM
AHHH!
HUFF
HUFF
HUFF
Y-YOU OKAY...?

YOU WANNA GO?!

COME AT ME, SEE WHAT HAPPENS.
UUURGH... WHY'RE YOU SO MAD?

BECAUSE WHAT DO YOU KNOW? BEING TWO YEARS OLDER DOESN'T GIVE YOU THE RIGHT TO LECTURE ME.
AND IF IT WASN'T FOR YOU, WE WOULDN'T HAVE FOUGHT IN THE FIRST PLACE!

HOW IS THIS MY FAULT—
YOU KNOW WHAT?
DUDE, JUST SAY YOU'RE SORRY.
IT DOESN'T MATTER ANYMORE.

AND FOR THE RECORD...
...I'M WAY BETTER AT GAMING THAN YOU!

WH...?

WHY, YOU...!
BAM!
GAH! CALM DOWN, KYLE!

WHOA...AND I THOUGHT AMY WAS TOUGH TO DEAL WITH...
SNIFF...
SHUT UP, ANDREW.

CHAPTER 8

MUNCH
MUNCH

DID YOU TWO HAVE ANOTHER FIGHT...?
NOPE.
NOT AT ALL.

THANKS FOR BREAKFAST, MOM.

Did something happen yesterday?

HONESTLY, I'M NOT SURE.

SEE YOU LATER, KIDS!
BYE, MOM.

HEY, GRACE—
YO! LITTLE GRACEY!

THAT WAS PRETTY AWESOME, HOW YOU EXPLODED AT KYLE.
LAY OFF, ANDREW.

WHAT, IS SHE STILL UPSET—
OUCH!
THAT'S ENOUGH, DUDE.

HAAAAH...

I DEFINITELY MESSED UP LAST NIGHT.

SEEING THEM WITHOUT ME UPSET ME MORE THAN I THOUGHT...

YOU COMING TO LUNCH, GRACE?
I'M STILL TRYING TO SORT OUT MY FEELINGS.

...BUT...

HEH. WHOOPS.

...I KNOW THIS SHOULDN'T KEEP GOING ON.

MY BAAAAD.

BUT I CAN'T HELP FEELING GUILTY FOR EVERYTHING.

MIND IF WE STOP BY MY LOCKER?

SURE, NO PROB.

SHOULD I TALK TO CAM ABOUT IT—

BUMP!

?

UGH...

WHAT A SHOW-OFF...

OH, C'MON. ISN'T HE SUPER-CUTE?

NAH...

?!

HEY, DOES HE HAVE A GIRLFRIEND?

N-NO... WHY?

REALLY?!
AHEM... I MEAN...I WAS JUST CURIOUS.
ARE THOSE FLOWERS...?

OH! HEY, MILA! OVER HERE!

NO...
WAIT...

MY KYLE-CRUSHDAR IS PINGING... IT CAN'T BE...
WAAAAHHHHH
WARNING, WARNING! CRUSH DETECTED!
WAHHHHH HHHHH
CODE RED! CODE RED!
IT CAN'T BE...

GRACE! WE'RE WAITING!
C-COMING!

IT'S ALL HIS FAULT!

MY EARS ARE BURNING...
Hmm
AAAND IT'S MY WIN!
TAB!
AHHHH...I WAS SO CLOSE THIS TIME...
HA-HA! YOU ALMOST BEAT ME.
JAY! I PUT SOME LEMONADE IN THE FRIDGE.
OKAY, THANKS, NANA!
LET'S GO OUT TO THE BACKYARD.
YAY!
AHHH...

IT'S BEEN A WHILE SINCE WE'VE BEEN OUT HERE.
...
REMEMBER WHEN WE HAD HOT CHOCO—
...JAY?
JAY!
HUH? WHAT?
ARE YOU OKAY? YOU SEEM LOST IN THOUGHT...
OH, I JUST...
IT JUST SANK IN THAT THERE'S ONLY TWO OF US HERE...
...OH.

S-SORRY, I DON'T MEAN TO MAKE YOU FEEL BAD...
NO, NO, IT'S FINE.

SILENCE~..
UM...

I MEAN...
...I MISS HER TOO.

BUT I WOULDN'T BLAME HER IF SHE NEVER WANTED TO TALK TO ME AGAIN...
I KNOW WHAT I SAID TO HER WAS REALLY AWFUL...

HONESTLY... I WOULDN'T BE SURPRISED IF YOU AVOIDED ME TOO.
WHAT'S WRONG WITH ME?

DON'T SAY THAT. I TOLD YOU, I'M OVER IT NOW.
I KNOW, I JUST...
...I'M REALLY SORRY...

IT'LL ALL BE OKAY.

THANKS, JAY.

HA-HA-HA!

SERIOUSLY, MY DOG DOES THE WEIRDEST THINGS!

I CAN'T CONCENTRATE ON THE CONVERSATION.

OH, DID YOU WATCH *IDOL TALENT* LAST NIGHT?

OF COURSE! THE THIRD GUY WAS REALLY GOOD.

WHAT SHOULD I DO IF CAM REALLY HAS A CRUSH ON KYLE?

YOU GOOD? YOU LOOK LIKE YOU HAVE A LOT ON YOUR MIND.

OH, IT'S NOTHING.

S-SO...

...HAVE YOU EVER HEARD OF A GROUP CALLED GET8?

I SAW THEIR VIDEO YESTERDAY FOR THE FIRST TIME.

IT'S NOT LIKE I CAN ASK HER...

THAT'S 'COS YOU LIVE UNDER A ROCK, GRACE.

HEY, ACTUALLY, ONE OF THEM LOOKS LIKE KYLE!

NAH, NOT HIM.

OH, RIGHT, THE PINK-HAIRED ONE?

HUH...?

THERE'S NO DOUBT ABOUT IT NOW...
I CAN'T WAIT FOR THEIR PERFORMANCE TONIGHT!
HEY.
HOW'S THE LI'L SIS?
THE SAME, I GUESS.
KYLE'S SISTER. YOU SHOULD'VE SEEN HER YESTERDAY.
WHO'RE YOU TALKING ABOUT?
THAT'S—
OH, THE ONE WE SAW ON THE FIRST DAY?
YEAH. SHE'S ABSOLUTELY NOTHING LIKE HIM, RIGHT?
YESTERDAY, SHE GOT SUPER ANGRY AT HIM AND—
DUDE!

THAT'S ENOUGH.

CHILL, DUDE.
OKAY, OKAY.
SORRY, MAN.

YOU COMING LATER?
NAH. BYE.

WHAT'S WITH HIM?

WHATEVER! YOU GUYS WANNA HIT THE ARCADE?
YEAH!
SURE.
KYLE, WAIT FOR ME!
ARE YOU ALL RIGHT?
I...
I'M JUST WORRIED ABOUT GRA—...
ONLY CHILD
EXTREMELY POSITIVE

...ARE YOU MAD AT ANDREW?
NAH. IT'S ANDREW—I'LL GET OVER IT.
HEH-HEH. I KNOW YOU NEVER STAY MAD AT HIM.
OH, PLEASE. IT'S 'COS I KNOW HE CAN'T HELP BEING STUPID.

CHAPTER 9

CHATTER
CHATTER
CHATTER

BUMP!

OOPS.
DIDN'T SEE YOU THERE, STEWART.

HEY...!
ISN'T IT GETTING OLD?!
...
HA
HA
HA
HA

SHE'S SO MEAN...
YEAH...

?
WHAT'S WRONG?
IT'S NOTHING...

I'M JUST... WORRIED ABOUT GRACE.
OH...

I HOPE CAM DOESN'T TURN ON HER...
HEY, GUYS!
HA
HA
HA
OF COURSE!
YOU'RE KIDDING ME!

YOU SO DID NOT!
BUT I DID!
HA
HA
HA
HA
OH YEAH!
Weren't you gonna ask her today?
WHAT'RE YOU GUYS WHISPERING ABOUT?
OKAY, HANG ON.
?
SOOO, GRACE.
YEAH?
I WAS HOPING YOU COULD DO ME A FAVOR...
SURE...?
I'M GETTING A BAD FEELING...
EEEK! OHMIGOSH, I CAN'T BELIEVE I'M ABOUT TO SAY THIS...!
JUST SAY IT!
AHEM-
OKAY, FINE. SO, GRACE, I WAS ACTUALLY WONDERING...
OH NO.

...IF YOU COULD INTRODUCE ME TO YOUR BROTHER!
THERE IT IS.
UM... WELL...
ARE YOU SERIOUS?
OH... HA-HA...
THIS IS REALLY HAPPENING.
S-SINCE WHEN...?
YOU'LL HELP, RIGHT, GRACE?
SINCE WHEN DID I LIKE HIM? IT WAS LOVE AT FIRST SIGHT ON THE FIRST DAY OF SCHOOL!
MAYBE YOU COULD TALK ME UP TO HIM!

PRETTY
PLEEEASE?

I...
I CAN'T.

...WHAT?
OOOOH...

WHAT DO YOU MEAN, YOU CAN'T?
I...UH...IT'S NOT THAT I... HEAR ME OUT!

I'M REALLY NOT THAT CLOSE TO HIM, AND I SERIOUSLY THINK THERE ARE BETTER GUYS THAN HIM... OUT THERE...
...

FINE. WHATEVER, I'M DONE.

HMPH!

C-CAM...?

CAM, HOLD UP!

WOW, SELFISH MUCH?

CAM, WAIT UP!
I CAN EXPLAIN...
CAM...!
HEY...
ARGH!
CAN YOU BELIEVE HER?!

I KNOW!
AND AFTER I WAS SO NICE TO HER!
SERIOUSLY!
DID YOU HEAR HER EXCUSES?
THEY WERE SO RIDICULOUS!
SHE KEPT FOLLOWING ME FOR, LIKE, THE WHOLE DAY.
EW, WHAT? THAT'S SO NEEDY.
YOU STILL GOING TO HANG OUT WITH HER?
OF COURSE NOT!
SCRIBBLE
ARGH!
HAAAAH...

MAN, WHAT WAS I THINKING?!

I'M SO SCREWED...

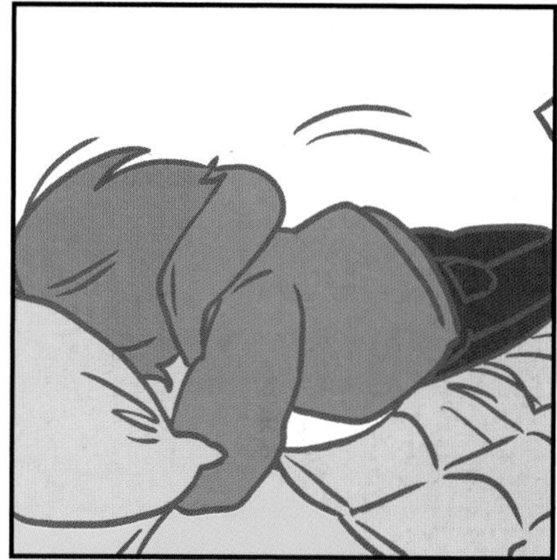

GAAAAH...
CAM SEEMED REALLY ANGRY AT ME...

WHAT WAS I SUPPOSED TO SAY, THOUGH? I WAS TELLING THE TRUTH...
I HAVEN'T TALKED TO KYLE SINCE THAT LAST FIGHT...
WHAT IS IT ABOUT KYLE?
IS DATING BETTER THAN FRIENDSHIP?
MAYBE I SHOULD HAVE STUCK WITH JAY AND AMY.
WOULD THEY ACCEPT ME BACK WHEN IT'S BEEN SO LONG...?
......
YOU IGNORED ME, GRACE. YOU DIDN'T STAND UP FOR ME.
HOW CAN WE EVER BE FRIENDS AGAIN?
AMY MIGHT HATE ME FOR ETERNITY NOW...

THERE'S PROBABLY NO GOING BACK WITH THEM...
I GAVE YOU A SECOND CHANCE AND YOU BLEW IT.

I'VE HEARD ENOUGH "EXCUSES."
...AND NOW WITH CAM TOO—...

...
BRIIING
OR...MAYBE I CAN STILL MAKE THINGS WORK WITH CAM.

HEY, CAM!
GOOD MORNING!
SO, UH... I WAS THINKING...

...I DON'T THINK I EXPLAINED MYSELF THAT WELL YESTERDAY. MAYBE—
HEY, AUDREY!

C-CAM?
MORNING!

......
OH...

BUT I...
SHE'S STILL MAD AT ME...
WHAT IF SHE CHANGED HER MIND?
WELL...
I THINK SHE NEEDS TO DO SOME GROVELING SINCE SHE TURNED ME DOWN ONCE...
...DON'T YOU AGREE?
HA-HA! THAT'S SOOO MEAN!

I CAN'T BELIEVE HE SAID THAT.
...
BRIIINGG
LET'S TRY ONE MORE TIME...
HI, GUYS! WANNA EAT LUNCH TOGETHER?
HMPH!
LET'S GO!!

...

WHAT'S UP, JAY?
...

COME HERE...
HUH?

WHAT?!
SHHH...
NO, CAM WAS TOTALLY IGNORING GRACE.
B-BUT ARE YOU SURE? MAYBE YOU SAW WRONG?

DO YOU THINK GRACE WILL BE CAM'S NEXT TARGET?
I HOPE NOT...

WE CAN'T GO TO A TEACHER WITHOUT SOLID PROOF...
TRUE...
IT MIGHT BE TEMPORARY TOO.

UNTIL WE KNOW WHAT'S GOING ON, LET'S KEEP AN EYE ON HER.

...BUT WHAT IF SHE DOESN'T WANT MY HELP...?

HMM...

YOU KNOW WHAT? IT'S FINE.

CHAPTER 10

BRIIINNG~...
THAT'S ALL FOR TODAY, CLASS.
LAST NIGHT'S EPISODE WAS HILARIOUS!
I KNOW, RIGHT?
IT'S BEEN DAYS.
YOU WANNA COME OVER TO MY PLACE THIS WEEKEND?
...
SURE! I'LL CLEAR MY SCHEDULE.

HA
HA
HA
HA
HA
I'VE TRIED TALKING TO CAM, BUT SHE WON'T LISTEN.
MOM WON'T LET ME BE HOME-SCHOOLED, WILL SHE?
SCHOOL'S NEVER FELT THIS BIG BEFORE.
HEY!
...
HA
HA
HEE
HEE
I'M HOME!
LIAM: YEAH!
HAAAH...
ANDREW: GOOD GAME TODAY!

KYLE:
SEE YOU GUYS
TOMORROW.
...
SO, UH...
HOW'S
SCHOOL?
...SINCE
WHEN HAVE
YOU CARED?
WHA...?
HANG ON...!

SLAM!!
UGH...!
WHY DO TEACHERS ALL GIVE HOMEWORK EVERY DAY...
HEY, GRACE!
!
H-HEY...
I COULDN'T FIND YOU IN THE CAFETERIA.
AND HERE YOU WERE INSTEAD.
...YEAH.
FINALLY! SHE'S WILLING TO TALK...
SO, UH—
HAVE YOU TALKED TO YOUR BROTHER ABOUT ME YET?

HUH...?
WELL? HAVE YOU?
UGH. GUESS NOT.

I...I THOUGHT YOU WEREN'T INTERESTED IN HIM ANYMORE.
ISN'T THAT WHY YOU WERE IGNORING ME THE WHOLE TIME?

OF COURSE I STILL AM! I THOUGHT YOU CHANGED YOUR MIND ABOUT NOT TALKING TO HIM.
THEN WHAT'S THE HOLDUP? WHY HAVEN'T YOU?
?
?
I DID, BUT...
BUT...
...I...
BUT YOU DIDN'T TALK TO ME!
BUT WHAT?

YOU... STARTED IGNORING ME...?!
YEAH, LIKE HOW YOU SHOULD TREAT YOUR FRIENDS.
NO, WE WERE GIVING YOU SOME SPACE TO THINK THINGS OVER.
TH-THAT'S... LISTEN...!

WHY SHOULD WE? WE DON'T HAVE TIME TO HEAR YOUR BORING EXCUSES.
GUYS!
IF YOU'RE REALLY SORRY, THEN DO SOME-THING ABOUT IT!
SEE YA!
Ha-ha! Did you see the look on her face?
...
I DON'T GET IT. WHY IS SHE ACTING LIKE I OWE HER SOMETHING?

AND THAT NONSENSE ABOUT GIVING ME SPACE TO THINK?

ON THE OTHER HAND, MAYBE CAM REALLY WAS UPSET...

BUT STILL!
SHE DIDN'T HAVE TO BE SO RUDE.

WAIT...

SHE SAID SHE FELL FOR KYLE ON THE FIRST DAY OF SCHOOL.
DOES THAT MEAN SHE APPROACHED ME KNOWING THAT I'M HIS SISTER?

......
NAH...THAT CAN'T BE TRUE.
AND THAT'S KINDA CREEPY IF SHE DID...

URGH... I'M NOT SURE WHAT CAM'S REALLY THINKING.
A?
B?
BUT I DON'T WANT HER TO BE MAD AT ME...

IS BRINGING KYLE INTO THE EQUATION THE ONLY WAY?
HERE YOU GO!
THANKS!
WILL IT SOLVE THE PROBLEM?

OH, BROTHER...
I HAVE NO IDEA WHAT I SHOULD DO...

BUT IT'S THE LAST THING I WANT TO DO!

WHY CAN'T YOU STAY OUT OF MY LIFE FOR ONCE?
FEELS LIKE SOMEONE'S TALKING ABOUT ME...
MY EARS ARE ITCHY A LOT THESE DAYS...
Have you read chapter three yet? I don't understand anything...
Yeah, I can explain it to you. It's not as hard as it looks.
Thanks! You're a lifesaver!
Hey, guys.

!
Hi!
Mind if I join you for a bit?
H-hi, Kyle...
So, uh...
How've you been?
Um...good! Actually...
Can we talk outside?
I was wondering if you guys know what's going on with Grace...
!
OKAY...SO BASICALLY, THIS CAM GIRL IS BEHIND THIS.
YUP.
WHAT DOES SHE LOOK LIKE?
REALLY CURLY BLOND HAIR, AND SOME FRECKLES.

WE'RE NOT SURE EXACTLY WHAT HAPPENED, THOUGH...
OKAY, THANKS, YOU TWO.
WELL...
I'LL SEE WHAT I CAN DO.
O-OKAY...

THUMP
KYAAA
GO KYLE~!!
GO!
RUN! RUN—!!
LOT OF SIXTH GRADERS TODAY.
YEAH...
CURLY BLOND HAIR
OMG, HE'S TOTALLY LOOKING AT YOU!!
FRECKLES

HOLD MY WATER.
?
HUH...?
YOU'RE CAM, RIGHT?
Y-YES!!
YOU BUMPED INTO ME IN THE CAFETERIA THE OTHER DAY.
Y-YES!
OMGOMGOMG, DID GRACE ACTUALLY TALK TO HIM?!
WHAT A CREEP.

ARE YOU FOLLOWING ME AROUND OR SOMETHING? IS THAT WHY YOU KNEW MY NAME?
AND YOU'D BETTER LEAVE MY SISTER OUT OF IT.
WH-WHAT...?
B-BUT... I...
LET'S GET OUT OF HERE...
SOBS... SOBS...

HOW COULD HE SAY SUCH A THING...?
HMPH...
I WONDER HOW HE FOUND OUT... I DOUBT GRACE WOULD HAVE TOLD HIM...
OF COURSE SHE DID.
HUH?
SHE CLEARLY BLABBED!
WAIT... I DON'T THINK...
I'M NOT LETTING HER GET AWAY WITH THIS...!

NERVOUS~...
EMPTY-....
THE COAST IS CLEAR.

I'VE DECIDED TO AVOID CAM FOR THE TIME BEING.
IT'S NOT LIKE SHE'D HEAR ME OUT ANYWAY.

SIGH-...
FINALLY, SOME PEACE AND QUIET...
BAM!!

FOUND YOU.

HOW...
HOW DARE YOU...!
WHAT ON EARTH DID YOU TELL HIM?
"HIM"...?

KYLE!
NOTHING...
THEN WHY WOULD HE CALL ME A CREEP AND TELL ME TO LEAVE YOU ALONE?
NOTHING? YEAH, RIGHT!
WHAT? WHEN DID HE SAY THAT?
YESTERDAY, IN FRONT OF A TON OF PEOPLE!

I WOULDN'T EVEN HAVE TALKED TO YOU IF YOU WEREN'T HIS SISTER!

ACK...!

WH- WHAT?

...I MEAN...
...
WOW. OKAY, THEN.

MAN, I CAN'T BELIEVE KYLE FIGURED IT OUT FIRST.

W-WAIT...
ENOUGH!
I'M DONE LISTENING TO YOU TALK!

I CAN'T BELIEVE I WASTED SO MUCH TIME AND ENERGY WORRYING ABOUT SOMEONE LIKE YOU!

GRRR...

...YOU...

YOU HYPOCRITE!

YOU THINK YOU'RE BETTER THAN ME?

YOU JUST STOOD THERE LETTING YOUR SO-CALLED FRIEND AMY GET PICKED ON!

WHAT?!

THAT'S...!

UN...
UNBELIEV-
ABLE.
WHAT JUST
HAPPENED?!
I NEVER THOUGHT
THERE'D BE A DAY
LIKE THIS...
PEEK...
KYLE BAILEY
ACTUALLY
STOOD UP
FOR ME.
SCORE!
THANKS FOR
THE ASSIST,
LIAM!
YAY!
WHO
WOULD'VE
THOUGHT?

DOES HE KNOW WHAT'S GOING ON WITH ME, JAY, AND AMY?

...I SHOULD TELL HIM THANK YOU.

HEY.
UM...
YES...?

ABOUT
CAM...
GUYS, I'LL
CALL YOU
BACK.
'KAY!

DID SHE
GO AFTER YOU?
I THOUGHT I TOLD
HER NOT TO!
SHE DID,
BUT I
HANDLED IT.

OH.
THAT'S GOOD,
THEN.

...WHY'D
YOU DO
IT?

WHAT
KIND OF
QUESTION
IS THAT?
WHY?
'COS YOU'RE
MY SISTER.
DUH.

EVEN IF YOU ARE ANNOYING AT TIMES.
UGH, OF COURSE.
IT WAS GOING TOO WELL.
...

OKAY, WELL. ENJOY YOUR GAME.
YEAH, SCRAM.

OH, BY THE WAY...

AMY AND JAY ARE PRETTY WORRIED ABOUT YOU. YOU SHOULD TALK TO THEM.
THEY'RE THE ONES WHO TOLD ME ABOUT CAM.

OH...
OKAY.
THEY WERE WORRIED?

BUT I THOUGHT OUR FRIENDSHIP WAS OVER...

~~
~~
DOES THIS MEAN THEY MIGHT TAKE ME BACK AS A FRIEND?

ACK!

WHAT IF THIS WAS A ONE-TIME THING?
I CAN'T BRING MYSELF TO LOOK AT THEIR FACES...
I WONDER WHAT KIND OF EXPRESSIONS THEY HAVE...
MAYBE OUT OF PITY?

MAYBE THEY'RE ANGRY?
I WISH SOMEONE WOULD JUST TELL ME...
NO, THAT'S NOT LIKE THEM...

ARGH...
I NEED TO THINK POSITIVELY.

WE MIGHT NOT BE ABLE TO GO BACK TO HOW WE USED TO BE...
HEY...
(AWKWARD ALL AROUND)
H-HEY...

...BUT I HAVE TO APOLOGIZE.

WHAT I DID WAS JUST AS BAD AS WHAT CAM DID.
AND I IGNORED JAY WHEN SHE TRIED TO MAKE THINGS RIGHT.

H-HEY,
GUYS.

I-I JUST WANTED TO SAY...I'M SORRY FOR EVERYTHING... AND THANK YOU.

I...
I HEARD YOU WERE WORRIED ABOUT ME, SO...
...YEAH.

THIS IS GETTING AWKWARD...
SO, UH...
...I GUESS I'LL LEAVE...
FIDGET...

HEY, WAIT. STAY.

YOU GUYS...
TOUCHED—...
WAHHHHHHHH
HMM?
ISN'T THAT THE GIRLS?
WELL, HEY! GUESS EVERYTHING'S BACK TO NORMAL.
HEH-HEH. ALL THANKS TO ME.
FRIENDS MIGHT FIGHT AND HURT EACH OTHER SOMETIMES.

BUT IN THE END, WHEN ALL'S SAID AND DONE...

...THERE'S NOTHING THAT CAN'T BE FIXED TO BECOME A BETTER VERSION OF ITSELF.

LET'S GO TO THE BOARD GAME STORE TODAY!

EPILOGUE

CHATTER
CHATTER

HEY, GUYS! YOU HAVE GOT TO SEE THIS!

HEY, AMY.
'NING ...

WHAT'S UP?
SEVENTY DROPPED THEIR NEW MUSIC VIDEO LAST NIGHT!

THEIR DANCE MOVES ARE KILLER! I CAN'T WAIT FOR THE ALBUM TO ARRIVE!
I PREORDERED IT MONTHS AGO!
MORNING, GUYS!
HI, AUDREY!
OMG, AUDREY!
HEY!
TURNS OUT AUDREY LIKES THE SAME K-POP BOY GROUPS AS AMY...
OH, HEY! AUDREY, RIGHT?
DID YOU SEE THE NEW MV LAST NIGHT?
OF COURSE! LOOK, I TOOK SCREEN-SHOTS!
...SO NOW WE HAVE ANOTHER AWESOME FRIEND, AND AMY FINALLY HAS SOMEONE TO FANGIRL WITH.
ALSO...

...CAM AND HER CLIQUE JUST IGNORE US THESE DAYS.
HEY, GRACE! WHAT'S UP?
I TOLD YOU NOT TO TALK TO THEM!
GEEZ, OKAY, SORRY...
WELL, MAYBE NOT ALL OF THEM.
HERE—
PASS!
PASS!
MY BALL—
RUN—
RUN!!

AND JAY, SHE SEEMS TO STILL LIKE KYLE.

I STILL THINK SHE'S TOO GOOD FOR HIM, BUT...

WELL, I GUESS HE'S NOT TOO BAD.

HIS ATTITUDE HAS CHANGED A BIT TOO.
GAH! YOU BEAT MY SCORE?!
AGAIN?!
SHOOM!
PONG!

HAH!
LIKE YOU EVER STOOD A CHANCE AGAINST ME!
DING!

OH, MY FRIENDS ARE HERE.
MINE TOO.

COMING!
DING~
DONG~

HI, EVERYONE!
'SUP!

HI, GRACE!
PIZZA
PIZZA
COOKIES

YAAAY!
WE GET TO SEE HOW GOOD THE NEWBIE IS!
I-I'M NOT THAT GOOD AT GAMING...
THAT'S OKAY, AUDREY, WE'LL GO EASY ON YOU.
MAYBE YOU SHOULD GO EASY ON A CERTAIN SOMEONE TOO, GRACE...
HEY! WHAT DOES THAT MEAN?

KYLE'S
LiTTLE
SiSTER
THE END

범이. (BUM)

BORN IN 2008

HI, GUYS! WELCOME TO THE VERY LAST PAGE!!
I'M BONHYUNG!
안녕하세요~
HANBOK
KIMCHI
KOREA ~
THANKS TO ALL OF YOU WHO READ KYLE'S LITTLE SISTER!
KYLE'S LITTLE SISTER
I REMEMBER HOW DARK GRACE WAS WHEN I FIRST STARTED THE STORY.
+ AND KYLE WAS THE NICEST KID IN THE WORLD.
OOPS

IT WAS QUITE A JOURNEY TO GET TO THE ENDING OF THIS BOOK.

AM
PM
GIMME FOOD HOOMAN
BUM
I PROBABLY COULDN'T HAVE FINISHED THIS RACE WITHOUT JUYOUN'S HELP!
EVEN THOUGH WE LIVE IN TWO DIFFERENT COUNTRIES!

PLUS MY PARENTS, WENDY, YEN PRESS TEAM + MY RIGHT HAND
YEN PRESS
MY FRIENDS

AND—!

YOU!

YES YOU!
YOU READ
THE BOOK!
THANK
YOU

감사합니다!

SEE YOU
NEXT
TIME!

GRACE

CHARACTER PROFILE

THICK EYEBROWS
ROUND EYES
ROUND FACE
MID-SHORT HAIR
Likes
•Playing Games
•Fantasy Novels
•Stuffed Animals
Hoodie Fashion
•Something Comfortable
SHARES SOME CLOTHES WITH KYLE
Hoodie Colors
Favorite Pants Style
•Pants with Lots of Pockets
NOT INTERESTED IN FASHION (YET)
Grace
6th Grade

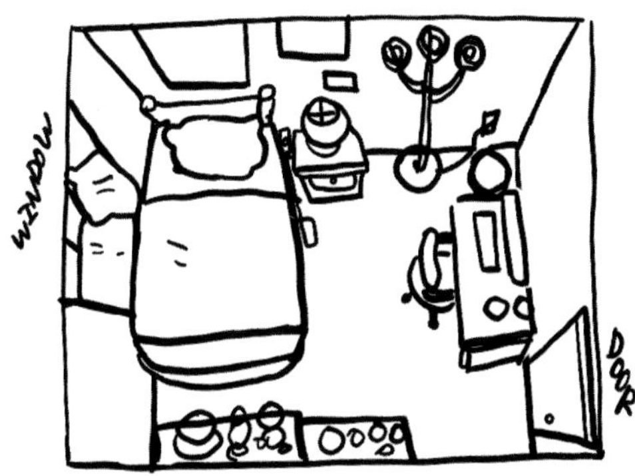

SHE LIKES TO SIT NEAR THE WINDOW

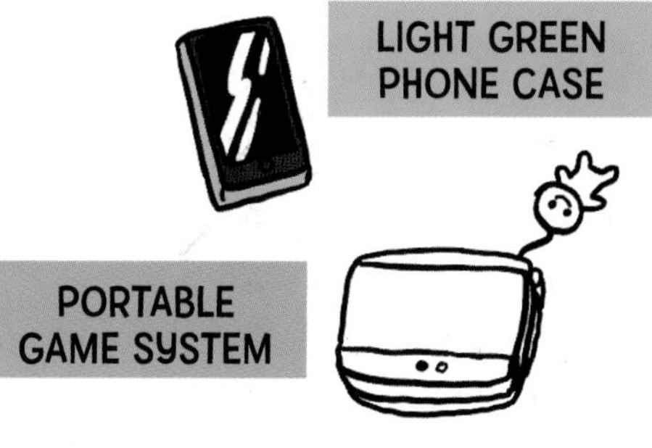

KYLE
CHARACTER PROFILE
HAIR DIRECTION SAME AS GRACE'S
THINNER FACE SHAPE THAN GRACE'S
THICK EYEBROWS
BASKETBALL BOY!
Likes
•Basketball
•Playing Games
USES SPORTS CROSS BAG AS DAILY SCHOOLBAG
T-shirt Color Changes
•Healthy
•Active
•Thoughtful
Kyle
8th Grade

GRACE PLAYS GAMES HERE WHEN KYLE PLAYS BASKETBALL

EXTRA T-SHIRT

BINDER

- PENCIL CASE
- WATER BOTTLE
- CELL PHONE

KYLE'S LiTTLE SiSTER
KYLE'S LiTTLE SiSTER
KYLE'S LiTTLE SiSTER
KYLE'S LiTTLE SiSTER
KYLE'S LiTTLE SiSTER